JACK

AND KILL

by DIANE CAPRI

Published by: AugustBooks
http://www.AugustBooks.com

ISBN-13: 978-1-940768-29-8

Original cover design by jeroentenberge.com
Interior layout by Author E.M

Published in the United States of America.

Visit the author's website:
http://www.DianeCapri.com

ALSO BY DIANE CAPRI

The Hunt for Justice Series
Due Justice
Twisted Justice
Secret Justice
Wasted Justice
Raw Justice
Mistaken Justice
Cold Justice
Fatal Distraction
Fatal Enemy

The Hunt for Jack Reacher Series:
Don't Know Jack
Jack in a Box
Jack and Kill
Get Back Jack
Jack in the Green

JACK

AND KILL

For Lee Child, with unrelenting gratitude.

1 CHAPTER

OTTO'S MOOD MATCHED THE bleak November landscape. They'd traveled the county road for eighteen miles under smothering gray skies, which allowed plenty of time for brooding. Thin snow covered the empty fields like a dirty blanket. Perhaps a riot of color had dressed the hardwoods before Halloween, but now only a few dead leaves dangled from dried stems beneath spindly branches. Even the vehicle in which they traveled was dull inside and out.

She felt captured in a monochrome movie. Yet, she welcomed the dreary weather because while the low, dense cloud ceiling interfered with the Unmanned Aerial Vehicle surveillance drones, she enjoyed a thin slice of breathing room.

Not the atmospheric gloom, then, but her quarry was responsible for her personal brain cloud. He was toying with her, which was okay. But he was winning the game, which wasn't.

"Tell me again why you think we'll find Reacher in New Hope," she said.

FBI Special Agent Kim Louisa Otto didn't mind matching wits with Jack (none) Reacher at the right time and place. Actually, she hoped this assignment grew in that direction.

Meanwhile, a better profile of Reacher slowly developed in her mind the way an old-fashioned photographic image revealed itself when blank paper was submerged in the proper fluids. She was better at strategic games than he was; Reacher's military file confirmed. But preparation was key. She needed to gather sufficient data to devise and implement a decent strategic plan before their joust. In short, she needed more time.

Meaning today was most definitely not the right day. Nor was New Hope, Virginia, the right place. Which was why, despite the perfect weather for a confrontation that might escape sophisticated surveillance, she wasn't all that happy right at the moment. She didn't expect to get any happier as the day wore on, either. She expected the opposite.

Behind the wheel of the full-sized sedan he'd selected at the rental counter in DC, Gaspar sprawled deliberately. His right leg was fully extended to reduce the pain that often hobbled him. Otto had stopped counting how many Tylenols he'd swallowed already, although she worried about his liver. One of many tacit agreements they'd fallen into during their brief but intense partnership. As if not asking meant not knowing, and not knowing meant not happening.

He glanced toward her and frowned, but his tone was quiet, perhaps annoyed. "I didn't say we'd *find* him, Sunshine. We're building a file, not conducting a manhunt. I said he was *there yesterday*. Big difference."

She could tell Gaspar wanted to find Reacher today, though. "Do I want to know how you acquired that intel?"

In response, he flashed a quick stare before returning his attention to driving. Which probably meant he'd ignored their operating protocols. Again. Working a different case with different rules, he might have offered more or she might have asked. As it was, they'd agreed plausible deniability might save them if either was eventually forced to testify. Which they'd also agreed was more than likely where the whole Reacher mess was headed.

"How much farther?" she asked instead.

He glanced at the odometer. "Maybe fifteen more miles. Give or take."

The rental was equipped with GPS and they had their own equipment, too. She could find the precise distance easily enough. But GPS acted like a tracking beacon for UAVs that crosshatched the country and she'd had enough of being watched. Instead, they did most things the old-fashioned way, making every effort to remain skinny straws in the very large haystack of surveillance data. The boss and too many others had unlimited access to their movements.

Maybe Reacher did everything the old-fashioned way, too. Maybe that was how he stayed far off the grid. It seemed if anyone saw Reacher it was not because they found him but because Reacher found them. Otto had begun to envy Reacher's expertise in privacy protection. He was exceedingly adept at secrets, too. Otto's experience said a guy that good at secrets had way too much to hide.

This county road would take them directly into town and no amount of reviewing their route would make the drive less desolate.

JACK AND KILL | 5

Kim murmured her thoughts aloud. "Why would Reacher come to New Hope, anyway? We've seen nothing but empty fields and this is the main road from the interstate into town. Not even a barn for the past fifteen miles. No diner with a good cup of hot coffee anywhere to be found. What the hell would he be doing here?"

Gaspar shrugged. "The guy's a psycho. Nothing he's done makes any sense so far. Why should today be different?"

Kim wagged her head slowly, as if clearing the cobwebs in an enclosed space to make room for better answers, but none appeared. "What's your plan if we find him?"

Gaspar grinned, stretched, flexed his shoulders and his neck. "You worry too much. There's no designated worrier achievement medal, you know."

She'd have punched his shoulder, but her arms were too short to box across the Crown Vic's wide bench while snugged into her safety restraint. "Just because I'm the one worrying about it doesn't mean the question isn't worrisome, Chico."

He seemed briefly startled by the vibration of his personal cell phone. Gaspar patted his pockets, arched one eyebrow to accentuate his words, and asked in a playful tone, "You really think we're gonna need a plan *today*, Susie Wong?"

Kim's concern jerked several notches higher when he retrieved the phone, glanced at the caller ID, tapped the answer button, and simply said, "Hello."

Gaspar's wife was very pregnant and dealing with four kids already. Although Gaspar kept the phone close at all times, Maria had never called before. Cops' wives rarely did because receiving the wrong call at the wrong time could cause disastrous consequences. No cop's wife ever rang up out of the blue with good news; no cop receiving the call ever displayed his fear when the call came.

Kim turned aside to allow what privacy she could within the vehicle's cabin. His side of phone conversations were mostly monosyllabic anyway. Kim easily tuned him out while she considered his point.

Even if Reacher had been in New Hope yesterday, experience told her to expect another dead end today. Perhaps she had missed something relevant. But what? She ran known facts through her head quickly.

Ten days ago, Otto and Gaspar were tasked with a routine assignment: build a file on a former military cop, applying standard background investigation techniques. The file would be used to vet him for an undisclosed classified project. Otto and Gaspar worked similar investigations as members of the FBI's Special Personnel Task Force.

The job had seemed feasibly straightforward at first. Some snafu somewhere needed ironing out.

Reacher's life was etched in bedrock government records like any other American from birth to age thirty-six, when he was honorably discharged from the Army. Up to that moment fifteen years ago, everything contained in Reacher's file was as expected. Records for birth, school, health, military, passport, driver's license, insurance, banking, and every other standard bit and byte of data existed precisely where it should have been.

The problem was that records simply stopped for Reacher at age thirty-six.

Otto and Gaspar were told to close the gap in his paper trail and bring Reacher up to date with the rest of the world. Something as simple as Reacher's death certificate would have settled the matter. Maybe it would have taken a couple of days.

Instead, everything got incredibly complicated very quickly.

Nothing about his file was normal now. Reacher's missing data traveled far beyond odd into unthinkable realms. Even when Americans were reported abducted by aliens, some secret government file somewhere existed to debunk the claim. But *nothing* for Reacher? Kim felt her head shaking, almost of its own volition. There was only one way such a thing could have happened in the real world whether Kim believed it or not; resistance was futile.

In addition, every normal resource had been declared off-limits from the outset. They were denied access to FBI resources, including personnel, computers, equipment, and databases. They had been specifically ordered not to attempt any normal channels because doing so would alert the wrong watchers. The boss delivered some line of bull to justify the straitjacket but his reasons didn't matter. Orders were orders. Rules were rules. The job was what it was.

Until someone tried to blow Gaspar into subatomic particles. After that, they'd started ignoring the boss's rules and begun creating their own.

Which was when they tried digging through back channels. Otto and Gaspar unearthed every file that might have held something, anything, connected to Reacher. Each time they came up empty—and pissed off somebody high up the food chain—they believed they were making progress. A confrontational warning delivered by Houston DEA Susan Duffy cemented their conclusions.

Whatever items remained so highly classified in Reacher's background were merely intriguing. Otto and Gaspar were comfortable with the concept of security clearances and lacking the requisite "need to know." That wasn't the problem. The total absence of those records was what worried Kim the most. Only a few highly-placed public servants had the ability to make so many routine reports disappear. And no matter how cavalierly he denied it, the gaping hole where the records should be worried Gaspar, too.

They now knew two things irrefutably and resisting the obvious was not only futile but foolhardy. First, someone inside government at the very highest levels had removed every piece of documentary evidence that should have or could have existed on Reacher for the past fifteen years. Second, Otto and Gaspar were being used to further someone's hidden agenda.

No amount of revisiting or rearranging known

facts invalidated these conclusions. Whatever she'd missed in her earlier analysis remained buried.

She returned her attention to the situation inside the gray sedan. A few moments later, Gaspar signed off his phone conversation.

Kim asked, "Everything okay at home?"

He shook his head and punched a speed-dial number on his personal cell. Holding the phone to his ear with his shoulder, he ran splayed fingers through his hair and expelled a long, audible breath. "Let's not go into now, okay? We need to focus on what's ahead."

Kim heard the robotic signals on the other end of Gaspar's phone line. Four rings later, a man's voice answered.

Gaspar grabbed the phone and held it close to his ear, allowing Kim to hear only one side of the conversation again. "Alexandre?... Yeah, still on the road... Look, I need you to do me a favor... Check on Maria this afternoon. Maybe get Denise to stay with her a few hours and help sort things out for me... Yeah, she'll tell you about it... Right. Turned himself in... Yeah, it's not great... Thanks, man. I owe you... Call me when you know more, okay? Thanks."

Gaspar ended the call and squeezed his eyes

shut a few moments. For the first time since she'd met him, Gaspar looked old and tired and in pain. He raked his hair again, swiped his face with his open palm, and readjusted himself on the seat. He sucked in a deep breath followed by a long, audible exhale. Another. A third. When his breathing settled, he said nothing while he navigated the Crown Vic through the too-early winter gloom.

After a while, Kim asked, "Do you need to head back to Miami?"

He cleared his throat. Voice barely audible, he said, "Let's do what we came for while my friends get Maria settled. Then we'll see where things are."

"Why not go now? I mean, what's your confidence level we'll find anything when we get there anyway?"

Gaspar sighed, stretched, tried to get more comfortable in the seat and with his family situation, whatever it was. Kim's gut said his efforts there were futile, too.

Wearily, he lifted the edge of his mouth in a near grin before he replied, "Just following the first rule of detecting, Suzy Wong."

She liked his weak humor. Maybe that meant everything was going to be okay back at home. She hoped. "Get a better sidekick?"

He cocked his eyebrow. "I thought you didn't want to know why we're headed to New Hope."

"I don't." Trouble was, she already knew.

Early on, they figured the easiest solution to Reacher's missing records was his undocumented death. Reacher was a dangerous man who seemed to attract trouble of the fatal kind wherever he surfaced. The most likely scenario was that someone, somewhere had been bigger, faster, and more lethal than he was.

That fantasy lasted almost eight days before Kim was forced to accept that Reacher was the farthest thing from dead.

In fact, she was almost certain she'd seen him twice in the past ten days.

A giant shadow in the distance. Watching. But definitely there was a guy, and certainly matching Reacher's description.

Gaspar hadn't seen him, but he believed Kim anyway. They'd agreed. Reacher was there. He was alive and watching. For sure. At this point, he probably knew more about Otto and Gaspar than they knew about him.

Their plan had been to find people he knew before he'd vanished and move relentlessly forward to uncover the rest of his story. Maybe spotting

Reacher watching them spurred this detour to New Hope; Gaspar probably figured to level the playing field by excavating more recent data. They had a chance to find Reacher now and they might never have that chance again or, at least, not for a good long while.

Which explained Gaspar's quip about the first rule of detecting: Follow the money. Money is an essential life force like air and water. Reacher's money had become relevant. Somehow, Gaspar had traced Reacher's money to New Hope. Kim knew several ways Gaspar might have exploited a weak link in the banking security system and she could imagine several more troubling sources of this intel. At some point, maybe she'd ask him. But she didn't need to do it yet.

Now they were uncomfortably close to Reacher's last known whereabouts. She wasn't exactly sure how she felt about that, but it churned her stomach like a thrashing snake. Not that her anxiety mattered. There was only one viable option. When there's only one choice, it's the right choice. Kim lived by that philosophy and followed where it led.

But they needed a plan. Just in case.

If they actually found Reacher today, Gaspar would need to do his job and, as the lead agent on the assignment, she wanted his head back on track. Knowing what little they'd already learned about Reacher, their very lives depended on being as alert as possible.

"Is there an airport in this town?" Kim asked. She noticed Gaspar's self-satisfied smirk, which meant maybe he'd begun to compartmentalize his personal issues if he was able to tease her. She hoped.

He said, "No."

"Train station?"

"Nada."

"Bus stop?"

"Nope."

"Car rental?"

"Doubtful."

"Taxi stand?"

"Unlikely."

"So you figure he's registered at a local hotel?"

"No hotels, either."

"He hitched a ride out of town then," she said.

"A reasonable conclusion." Gaspar waited a couple of beats before he replied matter-of-factly, "Or maybe a woman invited him to stay a while."

"So your plan is what? Knock on doors looking for women of a certain age, collect Reacher and invite him out for a beer?"

She was glad to see Gaspar grin, even if he was only seeking to lighten his mood more than anything. Lighthearted was better than glum.

He said, "Not *every* woman of a certain age."

"What's your criteria?" she asked, as if his plan might be worthwhile when she was fairly sure he was making things up as the conversation progressed.

"Only the good-looking ones."

"Models?"

"Who are single."

"Nuns?"

"And smart."

"Coeds?"

"And strong."

"Athletes?"

He waited a couple of beats for her to catch on. When she said nothing, he flashed her the look again. "And also cops."

The suggestion snatched her breath away. She felt her heart slam hard in her chest and her nostrils gulped air. She steadied her voice as well as possible. "Because?"

"Because he's a *smart* psycho. With good taste in women."

Gaspar's reasoning was sound, but she resisted.

"Two women. That's hardly a reliable pattern. And you're just guessing about Duffy."

He replied, "I know why I'm here. I'm a charity case." He slapped his right thigh with his open palm. "They screwed up. Now they owe me and they're stuck with me and I can't do the job. Don't waste your time trying to make me feel better. I'm grateful for the work, but I'm expendable. I know it, they know it and you know it, too."

The possibility slamming Kim's brain felt like a caroming racquetball. She'd given no thought to why she'd been chosen. She'd been too pleased with her luck. She'd developed a detailed career plan that included achieving FBI Director status one day. She needed opportunities to prove herself and this was one such chance. Nothing more she needed to know.

When she failed to reply, Gaspar said, "Take off your rose-colored glasses, Sunshine. You think the boss picked you because you shoot straighter than the rest of us? Not to be a jerk, but get a grip."

Kim didn't argue because his facts were solid and his conclusion flawless. She had no *particular* qualifications except that she was more expendable than he was because she had no spouse and no children. Albeit for different reasons, like Gaspar, her life belonged to the FBI and that was precisely the way she liked it. She'd tried and failed at love; she had no desire to travel that road again. She was alone by choice and she intended to remain so.

Could the boss have thought she'd be Reacher bait? The idea seemed preposterous initially, but had quickly assumed potential, almost inevitability. Questions popped into her head. How could she entice Reacher to approach her? What could she offer him? What was she expected to extract in return? Why wasn't she outraged that the boss simply assumed she would sacrifice herself when the moment came?

The answer to the last question was simple. She'd sacrificed herself for the FBI before and she would do it again. The boss knew that, she knew that, and apparently Gaspar had worked it out, too.

Kim was surprised to find herself so angry. "That's your plan? We find Reacher and lure him into some compromising position and then, what? Fall on our swords?"

Gaspar shrugged. Maybe he considered anew his problem in Miami. Or maybe he was giving Kim a chance to work out a better plan now that she'd faced facts. If she dared.

2 CHAPTER

THEY DROVE WESTWARD IN silence along the two-lane blacktop over hilly terrain another four miles before Kim saw the first group of modest homes lining the road on both sides. They were widely spaced and well kept, but only a few windows were illuminated from their interiors despite the dreary weather. Pole buildings, barns, and other indications of rural civilization seemed randomly placed according to no particular zoning plan for a mile or so until the Crown Vic passed a road sign proclaiming New Hope, Virginia's city limits. It also claimed to have been named an All-American city a decade ago, which seemed more than a bit ambitious for the collection of dwellings they'd seen so far.

The county road became Valley View, widened to four lanes, and the speed limit dropped to twenty-five miles an hour as they approached the town. Kim felt Gaspar tap his brake to disengage the cruise control. The big vehicle's progress gradually slowed along the tarmac.

Nothing obstructed her line of sight. Valley View ended ahead at a T-intersection with a landscaped ribbon of boulevard a bit farther west. A hundred feet before the intersection with Grand Parkway, Valley View sprouted a center left turn lane and a right turn lane and Kim observed traffic signals at each turning point. The signals for turning traffic from Valley View onto Grand Parkway cycled from red to green and back, but vehicles attempting to turn north were barely moving. Traffic turning southbound and eastbound was flowing slightly better, but without regard to the cycling signals, meaning cops she couldn't see from her vantage point were most likely directing traffic.

"Can you see what's going on up there?" Kim asked, glad for the excuse to resume normal conversation.

Gaspar stretched his neck and shoulders as he slowed closer to the bottleneck. "Looks like an old crash in the right northbound lane on the boulevard, doesn't it?"

"Hard to tell from here, but I'd say an hour ago, or more." Through gaps in the traffic, Kim saw a white Ford F-150 truck with a cap on the bed stopped on Grand Parkway about thirty feet north of the intersection.

The Crown Vic progressed haltingly along Valley View with no discernible rhythm to its forward movement. After a bit, Gaspar said, "There's a blue Toyota Prius's front end wedged under the truck's back bumper. That Prius is crunched up like it hit a brick wall at twenty-five miles an hour, but the truck looks undamaged."

"I'm counting maybe seven sets of flashing lights. No sirens, so yeah, they've probably been there a while. Blue, red, and white, but no yellow," Kim said.

Gaspar groused, leaned his head back and closed his eyes. "One day they're going to standardize emergency vehicle lighting in this country."

"Maybe. But right now, I'd say an ambulance is standing by, injuries were already dealt with, and locals are directing traffic and documenting the scene. But they've got no tow trucks to move the damaged vehicles out of the way, so they've got a snarl." Kim's mind appreciated the exercise of figuring out a simple, solvable puzzle for a change. Even though the solution was far from ideal. A tie-up at an intersection like this could take hours to resolve and she wasn't excited about spending the night in New Hope, Virginia.

"Seems like a lot of responders for a routine rear-end collision," Gaspar said without looking. "So you're probably right about the injuries."

Traffic continued to move slowly around the crash site. From time to time, Gaspar lifted his foot off the brake and allowed the Crown Vic to inch ahead. When they were close enough, Kim saw two uniformed police officers standing in the biting wind directing traffic, which was surprisingly heavy. They hadn't seen a single vehicle on the road in the hour before they reached the city limits. She guessed the bulk of New Hope's population must lie along Grand Boulevard. Or maybe this was rush hour.

There wasn't much to look at until they were allowed to make their own right turn and travel slowly past the crash site, craning their necks to watch the show along with the other gawkers.

Kim saw a woman, clothes bloody, shivering

under a too-small blanket, perhaps awaiting an ambulance. A towheaded boy, maybe about four years old and wearing a sweater and corduroy jeans stood a short distance away. Oddly for a crash victim, if he was one, the boy seemed to be chatting amiably with a uniformed policewoman. But it was the oversized mound Kim saw on the pavement covered by another dark blanket that caught her attention as Gaspar threaded the needle to move them beyond the scene.

"Pull over on the right," Kim said.

"Are you sure you want to do that? Even if Reacher's lying dead under there, we're supposed to be keeping a low profile, don't forget."

She didn't argue. Fifty feet from the official vehicles, Gaspar pulled off and parked on the wide gravel shoulder. They stepped out of the Crown Vic and into the stinging wind. The air smelled heavy with loam and exhaust. Humidity soaked her skin like a cold cloud bath.

"Aren't you Latin lovers supposed to be chivalrous? Why don't you ever have a coat to offer me?" Kim teased, shivering from nerves as well as cold as they trudged through damp earth toward the body.

"November's always great beach weather in

Miami and I don't own a coat." Gaspar had stuffed his hands in his trouser pockets after turning up his Banana Republic suit collar. "You're a liberated female from Detroit. What's your excuse?"

Kim wondered that herself. She made a mental note to stop at the first affordable department store. Surely somewhere in this town she might be able to find a coat to fit her, even if she had to shop in the girls' department.

Gaspar didn't dawdle even though his leg had to be cramped after all the driving. Kim struggled to keep up with his long strides. She didn't know the full extent of his injuries and he'd made it clear she wasn't going to find out more from him. Snooping into his background seemed disloyal; she'd wait until he trusted her enough to explain. He limped a little, but as they continued along he seemed to walk it out somehow.

First responders handled the chaotic scene appropriately, Kim noticed. Maybe this was a small town in the middle of nowhere, but officials performed as if they'd been well trained. Emergent needs had been attended to. Now they were processing the crime scene and handling traffic. No one seemed interested in the blanket or the body that lay beneath.

When Otto and Gaspar approached, a plain-clothes official standing off to the side noticed. He was a slim man, maybe forty-five or fifty, graying chestnut hair and thick black brows. He didn't ask if they knew the parties involved in the crash, but his tone was friendly when he said, "I'm afraid you folks are going to have to return to your car."

Gaspar waited for Otto to take the lead. Partly because stopping was her idea, but leading was also her job. She pulled out her badge wallet and held it in her left hand as she extended her right to shake, counting on the local guy to return her gesture automatically, which he did.

"Looks like you have your hands full here," Kim said, friendly too, slipping her badge back into her pocket. Now he'd have to request it if he wanted a closer look. Most times, they didn't. All cops knew an FBI shield at a glance. Gaspar didn't offer a glimpse of his. All cops knew FBI agents traveled in pairs.

"Chief Paul Brady, New Hope PD," he said, a voice that might sing tenor in the church choir. "You must have been diverted here, huh? Sorry to interrupt your work, but thanks for coming so quickly. Rest of your team on the way?"

Brady's words jolted her spine like a Taser

strike. Why would a local chief call the FBI on a traffic fatality? Sure, headquarters was only a couple of hours away, but the FBI's jurisdiction didn't include traffic crashes under normal circumstances.

Kim injected her tone with cooperative officiousness. "Why'd you call us?"

Chief Brady said, "I didn't initially. Witnesses said carjacking. Never been common around here and I hadn't heard the term for at least a decade."

Carjacking wasn't FBI jurisdiction, either, but Kim didn't say so. She figured Brady for a guy who had to tell a story in his own way and his own time. "Uh, huh."

Brady stuck his paws inside his jacket pockets. "The thing kinda snowballed. First caller reported a rear end collision. I sent a patrol unit out here to process that. A minute or two later, second caller said road rage. Said a huge guy got out of the truck with a shotgun. I quick dispatched another unit. Third caller said the truck driver bashed the Prius's window with the shotgun butt, dragged the woman out of the Prius and beat her with the gun like it was a club." Brady wagged his head back and forth as if he couldn't believe road rage would lead to such savagery, even though he knew it had. "When my officers arrived on the scene, they found the woman battered, the guy dead on the ground, and the boy screaming inside the car. That's when I grabbed my coat and dashed over here."

Gaspar shivered in the cold dampness, scowling as Brady's tale unfolded too slowly. Her partner wasn't interested in explaining things to annoyed colleagues arriving any moment. Kim knew because she felt the same way.

But she *needed* to see the big guy under that blanket. She didn't actually believe Reacher was lying under there. Not really. She didn't believe he'd been in New Hope at all. Not yesterday or ever. But one quick look would settle it and she was ten feet away and she wasn't leaving until she knew for sure.

Gaspar prodded Brady to get to the relevant facts supporting FBI jurisdiction. "Domestic terrorists? Contraband in the car? She killed him with an illegal weapon? Guy's a Native American?"

Brady's scowl matched Gaspar's now as the alpha males squared off. Kim intervened to avoid a stalemate, which would be worse than a skirmish at the moment. "You'd know everybody in town, Chief. Who are these folks?"

Maybe Brady didn't want a skirmish, either.

"Well, see, that's the thing. The Prius is a rental from West Virginia. The F-150 is a Maryland rental. We ran the plates. Both were picked up a week ago using a corporate credit card. We're running that down now, but we keep hitting dead ends on the paper trail."

"No ID on the deceased?"

"None."

"The woman?"

"Says her name is Jill Hill, but she has no ID, either."

"What about the boy?" Gaspar asked. "He looks like a little man who knows his name and address to me."

"He is all of that," Chief Brady's mouth lifted in a slight grin. "Cute kid. Charmed every one of us. He says his name is Brook and he's asking if the giant went to climb the beanstalk."

3 CHAPTER

KIM NODDED AND TOOK a deep breath. "Let's go see what you've got before any more daylight gets away from us."

She began walking toward the body, leaving chief Brady and Gaspar no choice but to follow. The F-150 and the Prius were almost bonded together at the crumple, meaning they had to walk around. Kim made her way through small openings between official vehicles attempting to block the crime scene from gawkers. Various personnel were milling around while they waited for the FBI to take over. Kim had no intention of doing so. Her immediate plan was to confirm that Reacher was lying dead under the blanket. Or not.

Depending on how this went, Kim might or

might not want to leave. Less than a minute later Otto and Gaspar stood beside the hulking mound. Her body hummed as if she were electrically connected to a power source. This could be him. The assignment would be over. She wasn't sure how she felt about that; nor did her feelings matter. It was what it was.

Gaspar asked a paramedic to remove the cover.

When they lifted the blanket, Kim required only the briefest glance to settle her questions. She glanced at Gaspar. He nodded.

His face was a mess. His nose was pulped and his cheekbones smashed. Hair was fair and long, hung over his ears and below his collar. He had the thick neck and heavy shoulders of a bodybuilder. His thighs bulged inside indigo jeans. He wore heavy work boots on his feet. The shotgun remained clutched in his right hand. Dead eyes stared at nothing. His forehead was red and swollen and might yet bruise, even though his heart had finally ceased pumping not long after he cracked his skull open on the pavement's edge. Bad luck, falling just there, where frost had heaved the pavement to a sharp edge harder than the guy's head.

No doubt he seemed like a giant to the boy. He was about 6'2" tall, maybe 220 pounds. The man really was huge. But not big enough to be Jack Reacher.

While she dealt with the adults, Gaspar approached the remaining eyewitness. Kim pulled out her smart phone and snapped a few photos before she asked the paramedics to replace the blanket. She noticed the deepening dusk and glanced at her Seiko to check the time. Soon, the official FBI team would arrive. She hoped they were bringing sufficient lighting. In another thirty minutes, they'd be working with only insufficient ambient light to process the scene.

She turned her attention next to the woman. Jill Hill. The name sounded silly enough to be real, but Kim figured it was more likely made up on the spur of the moment when someone asked and Jill wasn't prepared with a better lie. Because she had the phone out already, she snapped a few pictures of Ms. Hill, too.

Ms. Hill shivered under the blanket the paramedic had wrapped around her. Her blonde hair was matted with blood, probably from a scalp laceration. Scalp wounds bled like faucets. An effort had been made to wipe the blood from her battered, swollen face, but her broken nose was going to require surgery. Maybe her cheekbones were broken, too. It was hard to say given the lighting conditions. When she watched Kim, her pupils were uneven and nonreactive.

Kim was no doctor, but like all FBI agents she'd had extensive emergency first aid training. And what she saw alarmed her. She waved Chief Brady over and reported quietly, "She needs to be transported now."

Brady said, "We didn't think she was emergent. We were waiting for FBI to make the call."

Instead of asking why again, Kim said, "Now's the time." She understood the protocols for concurrent FBI jurisdiction. But if Jill Hill died for killing this man, Kim wanted that to be a decision made by the justice system and not the result when law enforcement failed to provide treatment.

Gaspar had crouched low, eye-to-eye with the boy, engaged in lively conversation. He was an adorable child who looked maybe a little familiar. Blonde curls, dancing blue eyes, sweetly cherubic cheeks, and a bubbly smile accentuated by a heart-shaped full mouth. Kim noticed only one odd note: Whatever happened here seemed not to have troubled him overmuch.

Kim tapped Gaspar on the shoulder. He looked up and she tilted her head toward the Crown Vic.

He nodded agreement. They'd been here too long. The unmistakable whap-whap-whap of a helicopter, no doubt bringing the FBI agents actually assigned to the case, grew louder. If they hurried, they could be gone before the official team disembarked.

The boy glanced at Kim and popped up wearing a drooling grin. "I'm Brook! You're tall as me!" he said, clearly delighted to find at least one adult occupying space near his vertical dimension.

Kim felt her back stiffen, raised to her full 4'11" height and straightened her shoulders before she teased, "In your dreams, Bucko!"

He giggled as if this was the funniest thing any adult had said to him today. Which, sadly, it might have been. He offered her a high five. She slapped palms with him, somewhat chagrined to realize that his hand was not so much smaller than hers.

Gaspar had struggled out of his crouch. "We've gotta go, buddy. I had fun talking to you."

Young Brook shook hands solemnly with each of them. Then he giggled his glorious laugh and waved while in a singsong voice he said, "Ta-ta! See you in the funny pages!"

"You bet," Kim replied. *Where have I heard that phrase delivered just like that before?*

They hastened toward the Crown Vic, not only

because of the cold, but because the whapping chopper blades had stopped.

Chief Brady stepped into their path before they reached the Crown Vic. "We sent a couple of cars to collect your team. They should be here shortly. We'll let you get right to it. Meet up later in my office?"

"That works," Kim said. "But you never told me why you called the FBI in the first place."

Briefly, Brady's brows joined over the bridge of his nose in puzzlement before enlightenment struck. "Why did we know about the kidnapping, you mean?"

Kidnapping?

"We recognized the kid from the classified BOLO." Brady chuckled like a proud papa. "He looks exactly like his grandfather, don't you think? What a charmer. This kid is likely to be president instead of vice president when he grows up, huh? He's already got the wave and the farewell line down pat."

4 CHAPTER

KIM FELT ABOUT TWO beats behind while she made the connection. Of course, the boy was former Vice President Brook Armstrong's grandson. That's why his farewell words seemed so familiar. Otto and Gaspar had been living so far under the radar, they hadn't even known about the kidnapping. Agencies would have been advised officially, but a media blackout would have been imposed until sometime later as a matter of national security. Kids of politicians were protected from the bright world spotlight. But FBI agents would have known.

Gaspar must have been similarly behind the curve because he didn't immediately jump in, either. Half a moment later, they completely lost their opportunity to leave undetected.

Chief Brady's gaze moved and fixed at a point beyond. "Here's your team now," he said.

Otto and Gaspar heard the lead agent speak behind them as she approached and moved into their line of sight. "Susan Duffy. Chief Brady?"

Brady nodded and shook hands and delivered a succinct summary, "Agent Otto here has already sent one injured woman to the hospital. One dead. And the boy is with one of my officers."

Perhaps Duffy decided to be discreet for the moment. She said, "Otto and Gaspar can catch me up, Chief. My team will come with you to the crash site. There's another chopper and team on the way to collect the child. I'll be right there."

When Brady and the other agents moved out of earshot, Duffy's congeniality disappeared. Her tone was as cold as the frigid wind. "Why are you here?"

Kim might have attempted conciliation if she hadn't felt like a complete fool. She hated being ignorant of a major alert for the entire national security team. And Duffy knew too much about Otto and Gaspar already. Belligerence was called for. "Same reason you are. Reacher. Where is he?"

Duffy didn't flinch. "You're confused, Agent

Otto. Building the Reacher file is your assignment, not mine."

Gaspar intervened. "You can do better than that. Maybe this kidnapping isn't our case, but it's not yours either, is it? You didn't tell Grady you're BATF, so he wasn't expecting you. Which means Reacher must have called you and that's why *you're* here. What are you worried about?"

Duffy seemed to consider things for a moment or two longer than necessary. Probably running the possible scenarios through her mind, deciding how much to reveal, what to conceal. Kim recognized the signs.

Duffy said, "Our team was deployed to assist with apprehension of kidnapping suspects and the continuing commission of federal crimes."

She'd chosen the option Kim would have selected and that was a comfort because it made Duffy predictable, which was the best thing an adversary could be. Kim would bet a month's salary Duffy's answer wasn't true, but it was vague enough. The kind of thing Duffy could maintain long enough to do whatever it was she'd come here to accomplish.

Gaspar raised his right eyebrow in response.

Duffy bluffed again, probably because they

were in no position to challenge her bluff. "You can check with my superiors if you like before you brief me on exactly why *you're* here. I'll wait."

Gaspar shrugged like a man who's played more than one hand of poker, too. "We were in process of our assignment when we approached what we thought was a traffic crash with bodily injury. We stopped to help. Now that you're here and in charge, we'll head out unless there's something we can do for you?"

Before Duffy had a chance to reply, an officer from Brady's team walked up, "Agent Duffy? The medical examiner wants to see you before they transport the body. Please come this way." Duffy simply followed; Otto and Gaspar tagged along.

The medical examiner was standing beside the covered body when they approached. "We've followed protocols, Agent Duffy. Is there anything special you want me to check before I go?"

"Identifying marks? Scars? Anything?" she asked, as if she thought there might be. Kim realized Duffy hadn't seen the body. Yet, she didn't seem to be thinking Reacher had found his match at long last and finally lost. She didn't seem worried at all.

"Unfortunately, no," the doctor said. "I've taken extra cheek swabs for DNA in case you have anything to compare at some point. But there is something I wanted to show you."

The medical examiner knelt down beside the body. Duffy tensed slightly and Kim wondered why; she already knew the dead man wasn't Reacher. Did Duffy know who the guy was?

He removed the blanket. He turned the burly man's head to the side exposing his ruined skull. "Cause of death appears to be blunt trauma to the skull caused by hitting the broken concrete. The curious thing is how his head landed here with sufficient force to cause this much damage."

"He'd fall pretty hard, wouldn't he?"

The doctor wagged his head. "I can show you the computer models later, but the short answer is that's unlikely."

Gaspar asked, "Meaning what?"

"Meaning he was pushed and pushed hard."

Kim felt what was coming in the same way she'd feel vibrations on a train track before the train appeared. Maybe Duffy felt it, too.

The doctor gestured toward the burly man's forehead. "See the redness and swelling here? If he'd lived, he'd have a hell of a bruise tomorrow.

He was hit with considerable force and weight, which knocked him backwards at significant velocity. When he hit the concrete the blow was much stronger than a simple slip or push and fall."

Duffy's face was a mask of objectivity. But Kim wanted firm, unshakable answers. "Could the woman have hit him hard enough to cause this?"

"I don't know for sure, but in my opinion, no. She's been described to me as slight and five feet, four inches tall. That makes the leverage wrong. I doubt she could have wielded any weapon with sufficient force to knock this guy down in this way, particularly in her weakened condition after he had already attacked her." He wagged his head again, "I don't see how any normal-sized woman could have done it."

"So you're saying someone else killed this guy?" Kim asked, to be clear.

"That's how it looks," he said.

"What knocked him down?" Gaspar asked.

"Hard to say. Something unexpected, because the deceased didn't see it coming and duck away. Something hard, heavy, strong. Not that shotgun we found lying there, for sure."

Duffy interrupted, "Thank you, doctor. Call me

from the hospital after you've seen the woman, please." She handed him her business card. Then she turned to face Kim. "Let's get a cup of coffee. It's freezing out here."

Otto and Gaspar walked behind Duffy the short distance back to the Crown Vic. As Duffy had foretold, a second, larger helicopter approached from the east, moving fast, rotors progressively louder, almost within range. Conversational tones became impossible.

Once all three were seated inside the car, Kim turned toward the back seat; Duffy's gaze met Gaspar's in the rear view mirror. She said, "You're looking thoughtful."

Gaspar started the engine and flipped on the heat before he replied, "Just thinking that what little Brook said to me makes a lot more sense now."

"What'd he say?" Kim asked, still watching Duffy. *What was she thinking?*

Gaspar said, "Brook wanted to know why the giant killed the bad man."

Duffy's scowl consumed her facial features like a plaster mask. "You've jumped to the wrong conclusions again. We need to talk before you get too far off the rails, which wouldn't be a good thing for any of us."

Still, Kim examined Duffy's reaction carefully, challenged. "You're saying Reacher didn't kill that guy?"

Duffy's sigh was barely audible over the rotors' noise. "It's not what you think, Otto."

Kim wagged her head with vigor. "Nothing about Reacher ever is." Neither Duffy nor Gaspar heard.

Gaspar's near-shout barely traveled across the increasing cacophony. "Why don't you enlighten us?"

Duffy projected loudly, "That's my plan. There's a diner on Grand Boulevard about a mile past the police station. Head north. I'll tell you where to turn."

Gaspar pulled the big car onto the northbound lane and joined the spotty traffic traveling now at normal speeds. New Hope was a tidy town populated with Disney-like storefronts and gaslights and lined with flower boxes still sporting fall mums in yellow hues. The sidewalks were swept clean. The only thing missing were shoppers, but given the weather and the hour and the excitement back at the intersection, an absence of pedestrians was not surprising.

Three miles beyond the crime scene stood a

freestanding red brick building with white Doric columns and an impressive double door. Once, it might have been a bank. Now, The New Hope Family Diner advertised breakfast all day. Duffy said, "Park in the side lot. There's an entrance there."

Also in the side lot were a dozen vehicles of various makes and models. At the end of the row, Kim noticed a standard issue government black SUV with dark tinted windows all around the back. The driver was clean cut, well-groomed, and infinitely patient.

Duffy led the way inside the diner and chose a booth in the back away from the other patrons. Duffy sat with her back to the exit, leaving Kim and Gaspar the best position choice. *Surprising,* Kim thought, as she and Gaspar sat facing the door.

After the waitress had taken their orders and delivered the coffee, Duffy said, "You've been out of the loop on this situation so let me fill you in first. The Vice President's daughter and her husband are divorcing. The divorce is contentious and not going well for her."

Kim had heard the rumors. Sally Armstrong had been a wild child when her father was one heartbeat away from leading the free world. Substance abuse was alleged, but never admitted. Marriage hadn't tamed her.

Gaspar watched Duffy closely while drinking his coffee, but he asked no questions, which was odd for him. His behavior had been erratic since his wife called earlier. Kim continued to worry about his Miami issues, but she could only handle one major problem at a time.

"Go on," Kim said.

Duffy said, "Six days ago, young Brook Armstrong III was kidnapped from his home in Arlington by his nanny, Jillian Timmer, and an unidentified man."

"Otherwise known as 'Jill Hill' and the dead truck driver I suppose," Kim said.

Duffy nodded. "Jillian had disabled the surveillance cameras, but she wasn't aware of additional surveillance inside and outside the Armstrong house. As a result, the Vice President's team knew fairly quickly that the two had abducted the boy. The kidnapping was well planned and well executed."

Gaspar wiped his hand across his face and made a strange, almost moaning noise. His voice filled with anger and accusation. "Meaning Jillian executed the kidnapping with the cooperation of one of Brook's parents, and you were one of the people supposed to keep that from happening, and then the team lost visual contact before they could be apprehended, right?"

Duffy's annoyance flashed, but she tamped down her temper. The effort cost her. "After that, we worked around the clock to find the boy. None of us has slept more than four hours in the past six days. We expected a ransom demand, but it never came."

Kim quickly put the timeline together in her head. "So you were working the case three days ago, when we saw you in DC."

Pieces of the puzzle were clicking into place, but what did the full picture look like?

Duffy had lowered her gaze and drank a few sips of black coffee before she continued. "We got a lucky break today. I received an anonymous tip—"

Gaspar's fist pounded the table, nostrils flared, a deep flush rose from his collar to his hairline. "Seriously? You expect me to believe *that*?"

A few diners glanced toward their table, maybe alarmed, maybe curious about the fuss. Duffy cleared her throat and continued as if he'd never spoken. "I received an anonymous tip a few hours ago. Brook was seen riding in a vehicle involved in an insignificant rear end collision here in New Hope. While we put everything in place to pick him up here, the truck driver got out of hand. You arrived before we did."

"What a load of crap," Gaspar said, angrier than Kim had seen him in their brief time as partners. Was he angry because of Duffy's lies? Or was it something else?

Duffy's eyes flashed anger now, too. But she remained seated. She drank coffee and, like Kim, waited for Gaspar to settle down. When he did, she handed them a hand-held video device.

"Press the play button," she said.

5 CHAPTER

OTTO AND GASPAR WATCHED the scene unfold on Duffy's video like a silent movie. The video was obviously spliced from images captured by several sources. The early segments were recorded by drones without soundtrack and maybe some kind of interior vehicle cameras. Later portions contained some sound and a bit of dialogue, indicating they were recorded by traffic cams and maybe other sources. The images were good enough. Clear enough to confirm some things. Not clear enough for others.

The sign advising sixteen miles to New Hope's city limits was four miles back on the road before the video's start. The hitchhiker was hunched into his jacket like cold and damp and heavy November air chilled his bones even as he trudged westward along the road's uneven shoulder at a warming clip. Stinging wind assaulted his face so he kept his head down.

Nothing to see, anyway. The bleak landscape was less welcoming than any Kim had traveled before, which was quite a feat. He probably felt the same.

Experience must have told him to keep moving until, maybe, the right vehicle came along. A farmer or trucker could have offered him a ride; maybe that's how he reached this point. Otherwise, he'd walk another four hours before he found hot coffee and a decent diner and, if he could muster a little luck, a warm bed for the night.

He'd made such trips before and Kim figured he expected more long walks down empty roads toward new towns in his future.

But Kim recognized him immediately because she'd seen him twice before. She recognized his clothes, too. The same heavy work boots probably kept his feet warm enough, dry enough. The brown leather jacket's collar was turned up and his hair covered his ears, but a cap and gloves would have improved things, weather-wise. Indigo jeans and a work shirt surely weren't sufficient. She wondered why he didn't wear something warmer, at the very least.

"That's Reacher, isn't it?" Kim asked. A test for Duffy. How far could she be trusted?

Duffy replied, "Can't see the face."

Which wasn't exactly true, but Kim figured Duffy knew the value of plausible deniability, too, and maybe Duffy's response was better than an affirmation for now.

"Why was he there?" Kim asked.

"I'm not a mind reader," Duffy said, a little huffily this time.

So she doesn't know why. And she's pissed off about it. Interesting.

Reacher looked less like a guy down on his luck and more like a threat, but there was nothing he could do about his travel costume then, even if he'd cared about fashion, which he probably didn't.

Kim wondered aloud, "Why was he headed to New Hope along that lonely road this afternoon? He was already here yesterday. Where did he go and why was he coming back?"

No one answered. Maybe someday, Kim would have the chance to ask him. She felt her stomach churn at the thought and controlled it by turning her attention back to the video.

Heavy clouds threatened snow to blanket the countryside again before nightfall. He could have slept outside. He'd done it many times before when he was in the army. But maybe he had a plan for a room in New Hope, although everything she knew about him said he wasn't much of an advance planner.

"There," Gaspar said, pointing with his chin, one eyebrow raised. "See it?"

She did. He'd picked his head up. His stride hesitated briefly.

Kim said, "He heard the car approaching when it was far behind him. Good ears."

"He's got years of training and sharp reflexes. And it was probably just quiet enough out there. The engine would've sounded small and weak and foreign. You can almost see him thinking it through, knowing he'd have trouble scrunching his six-foot, five-inch frame into the passenger seat."

Or maybe he was expecting the Prius all along because Duffy told him what car Jillian was driving, Kim thought. *Maybe that's why he there to start with.*

Gaspar said, "Alternative rides weren't thick on the ground. He probably figured nothing more suitable was likely to pass before nightfall."

A few moments later, Reacher had turned to face oncoming traffic and stuck out his right thumb, walking slowly backward, waiting. Kim recalled too clearly the biting wind that scraped her corneas. Must have been the same for him and caused his eyes to water, too.

He'd have watched through watery haze while the blue vehicle steadily narrowed the distance between them without slowing. Some optical trick might've made the car seem smaller as it came closer, which made no sense at all, but Kim had experienced that, too.

He blinked until his vision cleared, maybe. He saw a female at the wheel, alone in the Prius. Blonde hair. Nice face. Gorgeous eyes. Dark sweater. Maybe mid-thirties. Kim was shocked by Jillian's face. The face Kim saw after Jillian was viciously attacked by the truck driver, wasn't recognizable as this same woman.

Jillian glanced toward Reacher as she passed without slowing. Now, he blinked the water out of his eyes and closed his lids briefly.

"He couldn't have been surprised," Kim said. "What woman in her right mind would pick up a guy looking like him?"

Gaspar replied. "No woman should pick up *any*

hitchhiker, Sunshine. Not even you. And I don't care how good a marksman you are."

Kim didn't bother to defend against his challenge because she agreed with him on principle. But if Jillian had followed her first instincts and simply kept going, she'd be dead now. Maybe she'd known that. Maybe she knew that violence is a process, not an event.

After the Prius passed, Reacher turned to face westward again and resumed trudging, his head down against the frigid wind once more.

Less than five minutes later, he must've heard the puny engine's unmistakable whine again. He glanced up and saw the same driver behind the wheel. Maybe he wondered why she'd changed her mind. What did he think? Probably some misguided act of Christian charity or something?

The car passed him again, made a U-turn, returned and pulled up alongside. Jillian lowered the passenger side window and he bent over to speak to her. It was then he would have seen Brook belted into a booster seat on the passenger side. Young Brook's head was barely as high as the window's edge.

"What's going through his head now?" Kim asked, as if she was talking to herself.

"He's thinking she's either very brave or very foolish," Gaspar said. "What's she thinking?"

"Maybe she figured the boy would provide a level of security. She couldn't possibly have known whether he would hurt her or the boy, right? Was she stupid? Crazy? Both?"

Gaspar shrugged. "To him, her motives didn't matter. Hers was the only car he'd seen in the past hour and he was cold and tired and hungry. The only thing that mattered to him at the moment was getting somewhere to bunk in for the night rather than sleeping outside in the snow."

The boy grinned. His eyelids seemed heavy. A bit of drool dampened the side of his smile. Blue eyes widened when Reacher doubled over to stick his head in the window.

The boy said something. Reacher smiled at him, tried to look less menacing. No success.

Jillian shouted from the driver seat against the wind rushing in around him through the open window. Maybe she asked where he was going or maybe she just suggested he hop in. Impossible to tell from the silent video.

He said something. Pointed toward the town twelve miles ahead. He waited and she watched him a couple of moments, trying to decide, probably.

Maybe he was mildly curious about her next move. If a normal man had had any reasonable option, he might have allowed her to keep driving, collecting nothing but a story to tell her girlfriends about the hulking, menacing hitchhiker who'd flagged her down on the way into town.

He reached back and opened the passenger door quickly, maybe worried she'd come to her senses and speed away. He folded himself into the back seat awkwardly; his bulk barely allowed him to close the door.

The boy tried to turn around and look at him, but the seatbelt held him firmly in the federally certified and approved safety restraint system. Kim was glad the restraints worked because he should have been in the back seat. Brook wiggled a little bit before he gave up and asked his questions without eye contact.

Kim could see the child's lips moving, but she couldn't hear his words. "What did he ask about, do you know?"

Gaspar grinned. "He told me the whole thing, blow by blow. He wanted to know if Mr. Giant had a beanstalk they could climb. But it was a short conversation. Long on questions from young Brook and short on answers from the giant."

Jillian reached over and ruffled the boy's curls in a gesture as old as motherhood itself. She maybe asked him to be quiet and play with his toys. He seemed to do that and Kim saw no signs of unhappiness from either the woman or the boy. Had Reacher assumed Jillian was Brook's mother? A reasonable, if incorrect, assumption.

Jillian glanced into her rearview mirror to meet his gaze and spoke to him. Whatever he replied satisfied her because she turned her attention back to driving and soon had the car moving steadily westward again.

"What did she say to him?" Kim asked.

Duffy said, "I don't know. Maybe she'll be able to tell us when we have a chance to question her."

Reacher closed his eyes and dropped his chin to his chest.

Apparently, he wasn't in the mood for conversation. After a few contortions, he slouched further down onto the backseat.

"Is he sleeping?" Kim asked aloud.

"I would be," Gaspar replied.

Twenty-one minutes later the car had stopped at the intersection of Valley View and Grand Parkway, waiting for the traffic signal. The boy must have dropped something; Jillian seemed to be searching on the floor or maybe between the seats.

The traffic light changed to green, allowing westbound traffic to proceed. But the little car didn't move immediately.

Gaspar said, "This would have been the point where witnesses reported the first long horn blast from the F-150 immediately behind her car. Another long one, then two shorter blasts followed, Brady said."

"We've got spotty sound from here on out," Duffy said. She reached over to turn up the volume.

On the video, Jillian stopped searching for the toy and sat up abruptly. She slid the transmission into gear. Kim could see her lips moving as she spoke silently. Maybe she said, "Okay, okay, okay. Keep your shirt on. We're going." Or something like that.

Jillian pulled the vehicle through the intersection making a right turn and curving narrowly moving into the far right lane, allowing the angry truck driver plenty of room to pass. Kim heard his revved engine amid traffic sounds from other cars in the intersection. Jillian's Prius floated side to side in the truck's wash as it sped past.

And that should have been the end of it. In a

more civilized age, it would have been. But not this day. Because whether Jillian knew it or not, violence is still a process, not an event, and the day wasn't finished yet.

Instead, Jillian continued her steady stream of nervous chatter, but whatever she said inside the car was inaudible through the available surveillance microphones and the image wasn't the right angle for lip reading.

But the horns, the lost toy, Jillian's agitation, and probably a hundred other things altogether flipped a switch of some sort and the boy began to squall while still safely belted into his car seat.

Jillian glanced over, maybe to comfort the child. In the split second she was distracted, she didn't see the F-150 stop abruptly in front of her and the Prius slammed into what must have felt like hitting a brick building.

From the back seat, her passenger had no warning and no opportunity to brace himself. The impact threw him onto the floor in a jumble of boots and knees and elbows. Maybe his head took a resounding whack against the padded front seat.

Brook cried harder and Jillian panicked, yelling now, probably near hysteria, which fed the boy's squalling and the cacophony inside the car must have reached decibels assaulting all ears.

The truck driver moved swiftly from inside the F-150's cab to standing beside the Prius holding his shotgun by the barrel like a club or a baseball bat.

Kim and Gaspar watched Reacher struggle to extricate himself from his tortured position in the foot well. When the truck driver smashed Jillian's window, Reacher must have heard the sound of breaking glass and felt the rush of cold air into the cabin.

Jillian screamed and the boy continued screeching and while Reacher was still struggling to get up off the floor. The truck driver's angry tenor shouted, "What the hell is wrong with you, bitch?"

That was the point where the truck driver opened Jillian's door and hauled her out and threw her hard against the car.

Gaspar pressed the pause button on the playback to give them a moment Reacher didn't have at the time to think through the situation.

6 CHAPTER

BY THE TIME REACHER was able to assess the situation, chaos reigned. The Prius's front end had smashed into the rear of the oversized F-150 and crunched like an accordion. The burly driver, outraged, unrelenting, held Jillian by the arm and shook her, screaming angry words Reacher, still in the back seat, couldn't quite hear, either. The boy continued his hysteria in the front seat and the little car's horn, which had sounded constantly since the collision, blared as if its battery might last forever.

The truck driver raised the shotgun and brought the butt down on Jillian's shoulder hard enough to knock her out of his grasp and drop her to the pavement.

In a flash, Reacher propelled from the back seat,

over the wrinkled car hood, and when the burly guy raised his shotgun club again, Reacher grabbed the gun barrel, stopping the swing at the top of his arc and causing the burly guy's weight to shift and pivot on his left foot.

Surprise caught the burly guy off guard for a moment, but a moment was all Reacher needed. Briefly, their eyes met and the truck driver's bulged as if he was being squeezed by a bullwhip around the stomach.

That was when the burly driver made his final mistake. He faced Reacher full on and snarled a threat that seemed to faze Reacher not at all.

Out of the blue, Reacher head-butted him full in the face. Came off his back foot, thrust up the legs and whipped his head forward and smashed it into the guy's nose, like hitting him in the face with a bowling ball.

His legs crumpled and he hit the floor like a puppet with the strings cut.

And his head cracked on the concrete's jagged edge.

When the truck driver went down and stayed down, Reacher moved swiftly to Jillian's side. He helped her to her feet, steadied her inside the Prius, then knelt to talk with her, watching her face carefully, maybe looking for the non-reactive pupils Kim saw hours later. They exchanged a few words the microphones didn't catch, but it seemed like a brief and gentle disagreement.

Jillian waved toward the moving traffic. A few vehicles had slowed and some had stopped. A man held a cell phone to his ear. A woman dressed in nurse's garb approached to help. Jillian glanced at Reacher once more and a long look communicating something unspoken passed between them.

More cars slowed, stopped, and people came to help.

Reacher stood, turned, and walked northward along Grand Boulevard's gravel shoulder. In the final moments of the video, his image was grainy, indistinct. Perhaps another drone camera's capture or maybe Duffy had cut the sound.

Reacher seemed to have a cell phone held to his ear. Then he dropped it onto the pavement and crushed it with the heel of his boot before he turned, stuck out his thumb, and waited for a ride.

The video ended. Silence reigned while the three agents mulled things over.

Duffy said, "I'm going to the restroom. I'll be right back." She picked up the video player and left the table.

Gaspar said, "I have to call Maria." He left the table, too, and Kim heard, "Alexandre? How is she?" before he moved through the front door of The New Hope Family Diner in search of a better signal.

7 CHAPTER

KIM REMAINED SEATED, TRYING to make sense of the puzzle picture and Reacher's jumbled profile as Duffy's video destroyed the working hypothesis she'd formed in her head.

Several things that had been mysteries a few hours ago were now solved. Duffy had done Reacher a favor three days ago when she warned Otto and Gaspar to stop digging for Reacher's records. Reacher probably came to New Hope to return that favor.

He figured somehow that Jillian Timmer and Brook Armstrong were hiding here. Reacher discovered or deduced a connection between Jillian and New Hope, even if Duffy didn't know what it was yet. Maybe she or Kim would find the connection, but it didn't really matter now that the kidnapping was resolved and Reacher had obviously moved on.

Maybe Reacher had planned to kill the truck driver and maybe not. Either way would no doubt have been fine with Reacher.

The confounding point was his motivation. Was it possible that all he wanted was to release Jillian from the man's hold and help Duffy return Brook to his family?

Gaspar returned to the table, smiling a little, Kim thought. "Maria doing better?"

"She's got a ways to go, but thank God for Alexandre and Denise. They're staying with her, helping with the kids until I can get back. I'll tell you about it later. Where's Duffy?"

Kim looked out into the parking lot and noticed that the black SUV with the tinted windows and government plates was gone.

THE END

AUTHOR'S NOTE

I hope you enjoyed *Jack and Kill* as much as I enjoyed writing it for you. I hope you'll recommend my books to your friends who might like them, too. The best way to share your honest review of my books is to post a quick two or three sentence review where you bought this copy and give the books some stars. Please do that. I promise I won't forget it! And now that we've found each other, let's keep in touch. Readers like you are the reason I write!

More adventures with Otto and Gaspar on the Hunt For Jack Reacher coming soon!

Want to find out how The Hunt for Jack Reacher began?

Read on for an excerpt of

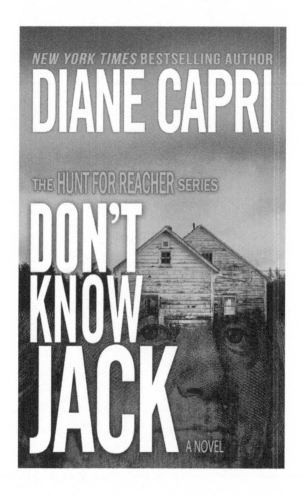

CHAPTER ONE

Monday, November 1
4:00 a.m.
Detroit, Michigan

JUST THE FACTS. AND not many of them, either. Jack Reacher's file was too stale and too thin to be credible. No human could be as invisible as Reacher appeared to be, whether he was currently above the ground or under it. Either the file had been sanitized, or Reacher was the most off-the-grid paranoid Kim Otto had ever heard of.

What had she missed?

At four in the morning the untraceable cell phone had vibrated on her bedside table. She had slept barely a hundred minutes. She cleared her throat, grabbed the phone, flipped it open, swung her legs out of bed, and said, "FBI Special Agent Kim Otto."

The man said, "I'm sorry to call you so early, Otto."

She recognized the voice, even though she hadn't heard it for many years. He was still polite. Still undemanding. He didn't need to be demanding. His every request was always granted. No one thwarted him in any way for any reason. Ever.

She said, "I was awake." She was lying, and she knew he knew it, and she knew he didn't care. He was the boss. And she owed him.

She walked across the bedroom and flipped on the bathroom light. It was harsh. She grimaced at herself in the mirror and splashed cold water on her face. She felt like she'd tossed back a dozen tequila shots last night, and she was glad that she hadn't.

The voice asked, "Can you be at the airport for the 5:30 flight to Atlanta?"

"Of course." Kim answered automatically, and set her mind to making it happen.

Showered, dressed, and seated on a plane in ninety minutes? Easy. Her apartment stood ten blocks from the FBI's Detroit Field Office, where a helicopter waited, ever ready. She picked up her personal cell and began texting the duty pilot to meet her at the helipad in twenty. From the pad to the airport was a quick fifteen. She'd have time to spare.

But as if he could hear her clicking the silent keys, he said, "No helicopter. Keep this under the radar. Until we know what we're dealing with, that is."

The direct order surprised her. Too blunt. No wiggle room. Uncharacteristic. Coming from anyone lower down the food chain, the order might have been illegal, too.

"Of course," Kim said again. "I understand. Under the radar. No problem." She hit the delete button on the half-finished text. He hadn't said undercover.

The FBI operated in the glare of every possible spotlight. Keeping something under the radar added layers of complication. Under the radar meant no official recognition. No help, either. Off the books. She didn't have to hide, but she'd need to be careful what she revealed and to whom. Agents died during operations under the radar. Careers were killed there, too. So Otto heeded her internal warning system and placed herself on security alert, level red. She didn't ask to whom she'd report because she already knew. He wouldn't have called her directly if he intended her to report through normal channels. Instead, she turned her mind to solving the problem at hand.

How could she possibly make a commercial flight scheduled to depart—she glanced at the bedside clock—in eighty-nine minutes? There was no reliable subway or other public transportation in the Motor City. A car was the only option, through traffic and construction. Most days it took ninety minutes door to door, just to reach the airport.

She now had eighty-eight.

And she was still standing naked in her bathroom.

Only one solution. There was a filthy hot sheets motel three blocks away specializing in hourly racks for prostitutes and drug dealers. Her office handled surveillance of terrorists who stopped there after crossing the Canadian border from Windsor. Gunfire was a nightly occurrence. But a line of cabs always stood outside, engines running, because tips there were good. One of those cabs might get her to the flight on time. She shivered.

"Agent Otto?" His tone was calm. "Can you make it? Or do we need to hold the plane?"

She heard her mother's voice deep in her reptile brain: *When there's only one choice, it's the right choice.*

"I'll be out the door in ten minutes," she told him, staring down her anxiety in the mirror.

"Then I'll call you back in eleven."

She waited for dead air. When it came, she grabbed her toothbrush and stepped into shower water pumped directly out of the icy Detroit River. The cold spray warmed her frigid skin.

SEVEN MINUTES LATER—OUT of breath, heart pounding—she was belted into the back seat of a filthy taxi. The driver was an Arab. She told him she'd pay double if they reached the Delta terminal in under an hour.

"Yes, of course, miss," he replied, as if the request was standard for his enterprise, which it probably was.

She cracked the window. Petroleum-heavy air hit her face and entered her lungs and chased away the more noxious odors inside the cab. She patted her sweatsuit pocket to settle the cell phone more comfortably against her hip.

Twenty past four in the morning, Eastern

Daylight Time. Three hours before sunrise. The moon was not bright enough to lighten the blackness, but the street lamps helped. Outbound traffic crawled steadily. Night construction crews would be knocking off in forty minutes. No tie-ups, maybe. God willing.

Before the phone vibrated again three minutes later, she'd twisted her damp black hair into a low chignon, swiped her lashes with mascara and her lips with gloss, dabbed blush on her cheeks, and fastened a black leather watch-band onto her left wrist. She needed another few minutes to finish dressing. Instead, she pulled the cell from her pocket. While she remained inside the cab, she reasoned, he couldn't see she was wearing only a sweatsuit, clogs, and no underwear.

This time, she didn't identify herself when she answered and kept her responses brief. Taxi drivers could be exactly what they seemed, but Kim Otto didn't take unnecessary risks, especially on alert level red.

She took a moment to steady her breathing before she answered calmly, "Yes."

"Agent Otto?" he asked, to be sure, perhaps.

"Yes, sir."

"They'll hold the plane. No boarding pass

required. Flash your badge through security. A TSA officer named Kaminsky is expecting you."

"Yes, sir." She couldn't count the number of laws she'd be breaking. The paperwork alone required to justify boarding a flight in the manner he had just ordered would have buried her for days. Then she smiled. No paperwork this time. The idea lightened her mood. She could grow to like under the radar work.

He said, "You need to be at your destination on time. Not later than eleven thirty this morning. Can you make that happen?"

She thought of everything that could go wrong. The possibilities were endless. They both knew she couldn't avoid them all. Still, she answered, "Yes, sir, of course."

"You have your laptop?"

"Yes, sir, I do." She glanced at the case to confirm once more that she hadn't left it behind when she rushed out of her apartment.

"I've sent you an encrypted file. Scrambled signal. Download it now, before you reach monitored airport communication space."

"Yes, sir."

There was a short pause, and then he said, "Eleven thirty, remember. Don't be late."

She interpreted urgency in his repetition. She said, "Right, sir." She waited for dead air again before she closed the phone and returned it to her pocket. Then she lifted her Bureau computer from the floor and pressed the power switch. It booted up in fourteen seconds, which was one fewer than the government had spent a lot of money to guarantee.

The computer found the secure satellite, and she downloaded the encrypted file. She moved it to a folder misleadingly labeled *Non-work Miscellaneous* and closed the laptop. No time to read now. She noticed her foot tapping on the cab's sticky floor. She couldn't be late. No excuses.

Late for what?

FROM LEE CHILD
THE REACHER REPORT:
March 2nd, 2012

The other big news is Diane Capri—a friend of mine—wrote a book revisiting the events of KILLING FLOOR in Margrave, Georgia. She imagines an FBI team tasked to trace Reacher's current-day whereabouts. They begin by interviewing people who knew him—starting out with Roscoe and Finlay. Check out this review: "Oh heck yes! I am in love with this book. I'm a huge Jack Reacher fan. If you don't know Jack (pun intended!) then get thee to the bookstore/wherever you buy your fix and pick up one of the many Jack Reacher books by Lee Child. Heck, pick up all of them. In particular, read Killing Floor. Then come back and read Don't Know Jack. This story picks up the other from the point of view of Kim and Gaspar, FBI agents assigned to build a file on Jack Reacher. The problem is, as anyone who knows Reacher can attest, he lives completely off the grid. No cell phone, no house, no car...he's not tied down. A pretty daunting task, then, wouldn't you say?

First lines: "Just the facts. And not many of them, either. Jack Reacher's file was too stale and too thin to be credible. No human could be as invisible as Reacher appeared to be, whether he was currently above the ground or under it. Either the file had been sanitized, or Reacher was the most off-the-grid paranoid Kim Otto had ever heard of." Right away, I'm sensing who Kim Otto is and I'm delighted that I know something she doesn't. You see, I DO know Jack. And I know he's not paranoid. Not really. I know why he lives as he does, and I know what kind of man he is. I loved having that over Kim and Gaspar. If you haven't read any Reacher novels, then this will feel like a good, solid story in its own right. If you have...oh if you have, then you, too, will feel like you have a one-up on the FBI. It's a fun feeling!

"Kim and Gaspar are sent to Margrave by a mysterious boss who reminds me of Charlie, in Charlie's Angels. You never see him...you hear him. He never gives them all the facts. So they are left with a big pile of nothing. They end up embroiled in a murder case that seems connected to Reacher somehow, but they can't see how. Suffice to say the efforts to find the murderer, and Reacher, and not lose their own heads in the process, makes for an entertaining read.

"I love the way the author handled the entire story. The pacing is dead on (ok another pun intended), the story is full of twists and turns like a Reacher novel would be, but it's another viewpoint of a Reacher story. It's an outside-in approach to Reacher.

"You might be asking, do they find him? Do they finally meet the infamous Jack Reacher?

"Go...read...now...find out!"

Sounds great, right? Check out "Don't Know Jack," and let me know what you think.

So that's it for now ... again, thanks for reading THE AFFAIR, and I hope you'll like A WANTED MAN just as much in September.

Lee Child

ABOUT THE AUTHOR

Diane Capri is a *New York Times*, *USA Today*, and worldwide bestselling author.

She's a recovering lawyer and snowbird who divides her time between Florida and Michigan. An active member of Mystery Writers of America, Author's Guild, International Thriller Writers, Alliance of Independent Authors, and Sisters in Crime, she loves to hear from readers and is hard at work on her next novel.

Please connect with her online:

Website: http://www.DianeCapri.com
Twitter: http://twitter.com/@DianeCapri
Facebook: http://www.facebook.com/Diane.Capri1
http://www.facebook.com/DianeCapriBooks

If you would like to be kept up to date with infrequent email including release dates for Diane Capri books, free offers, gifts, and general information for members only, please sign up for our Diane Capri Crowd mailing list. We don't want to leave you out! Sign up here:

http://dianecapri.com/contact/

Made in the USA
Coppell, TX
17 April 2021

53932352R00059